Nasty Kyle the Crocodile

Doug Cushman

Publishers • GROSSET & DUNLAP • New York

CONTENTS

For Zach, Lejo, and Pookie

Published simultaneously in Canada. Printed in the United States of America. ISBN: 0-448-16592-9. Library of Congress Catalog Card Number: 83-47681.

KYLE PAINTS HIS HOUSE

Nasty Kyle the Crocodile lives alone with his banded mongoose and a spider plant.

Kyle is a grouch most of the time. He hates things for the silliest reasons.

Kyle doesn't like eggs, because they have shells, or peanuts because they are crunchy.

Kyle doesn't like typewriters, because they can't spell, or birthdays for no real reason at all.

Kyle doesn't like the weather much, either.
"It's too wet," he grumbles when it rains.

"It's too cold," he grumbles when it snows.

One sunny morning after Kyle grumbled, "It's too hot," he dragged a ladder from his garage and began to paint his house. He decided to paint it BLUE.

Fred Goat, out on his morning stroll, said, "My! What a beautiful BLUE! You'll have the best-looking house on the block, I'm sure!"

"Yuk!" Kyle said. "I hate compliments. I'm going to change colors." He pulled out a can of RED paint and began painting again.

Olivia Hippo, on her way to the bakery, exclaimed, "Oh! RED is my favorite color! You'll have a lovely house when you're through."

"Aarrgh!" said Kyle. "I hate compliments!" He brought out a can of YELLOW paint and continued painting.

"What a bright, happy color," said Suzy Koala from next door. "I love YELLOW."

"I hate happy colors," grumbled Kyle. He mixed his BLUE paint and his YELLOW paint and made GREEN. He started painting again.

The little pig twins, Max and Flax, argued whether they liked GREEN or YELLOW best. Kyle mixed the RED paint and the YELLOW paint together to make ORANGE and mixed the RED paint with BLUE to make PURPLE. He worked with two paintbrushes for the rest of the day.

When Kyle finally came down from his ladder and looked at his house, this is what he saw!

"Aarrgh!" Kyle cried. "My house looks so horrible even *I* don't like it. But then no one else will, either. So I'll leave it the way it is."

The next morning Kyle woke up to the sound of his neighbors talking outside.

"What a wonderful house," they said. "So colorful. It's the best house on the block."

"Yuk," grumbled Kyle, but he was too tired to argue.

KYLE SHOVELS SOME SNOW

Kyle woke up one winter morning and discovered his driveway was covered with snow. So he trudged out to the garage to look for his snow shovel.

"Rats!" Kyle complained. "I hate shoveling snow." He took two steps backwards and tripped over his hoe.

"Aarrgh!" Kyle cried. "I hate planting my garden in the spring." Kyle turned and stepped on his rake.

"Ouch!" he yelled. "And I hate raking leaves in the fall." The garden hose fell off its peg.

"I hate watering the grass in the summer," Kyle cried. "I hate *all* the seasons. There's too much work when things keep changing. I want all the seasons to be the same!"

The garage door opened, and in walked Uncle Miles dressed in his best skiing outfit.

"Hi, Kyle," he said. "Let's go skiing."

"I hate the snow," complained Kyle. "I want to go where it's the same every day, all year round."

"Hmm," said Uncle Miles. "That may be difficult. But if we think hard enough we may find somewhere you could go."

“You could try the North Pole,” said Uncle Miles. “It’s always cold there. You would live in an igloo and catch your dinner through a hole in your floor. It would be the same every day. You wouldn’t have to worry about it ever getting warm enough for swimming or eating hot dogs at a baseball game in the park.”

“Hmph!” said Kyle. “The North Pole wouldn’t be any good.”

"Well, then," said Uncle Miles, "maybe you could go to a rain forest. That's always the same, with lots of nice, hot steamy days. You would sleep outside in a hammock and never have to wear a coat. Of course, you couldn't build a snowman or go ice skating on the pond, or..."

"Drink hot chocolate," said Kyle. "No, I wouldn't like it there."

"How about the desert?" suggested Miles. "It's always the same there. You could ride your camel through lots and lots of sand. The sun is always shining. In the desert you wouldn't have to bother with planting your garden and watching beautiful flowers grow. Nope, no red roses to water and green grass to mow in the desert."

"It's pretty hot in the desert," said Kyle. "I don't think I want to go there."

"You could go to a South Sea island," said Uncle Miles. "It's always warm there, and it would always be green everywhere you looked. You wouldn't have to rake the leaves, because they wouldn't turn pretty colors in the fall."

"And I couldn't go trick-or-treating," said Kyle sadly.

"No," said Miles, "but there is one place where you can ice skate in the winter, plant a garden in the spring, swim in the summer, and watch the leaves turn in the fall."

"Where?" asked Kyle.

"Right here at home," said Miles.

"I suppose the seasons aren't so bad," said Kyle. "You can always do something different."

"Right," said Miles. "Instead of skiing, let's go outside and make snow angels."

"Last one outside is a rotten egg!" yelled Kyle.

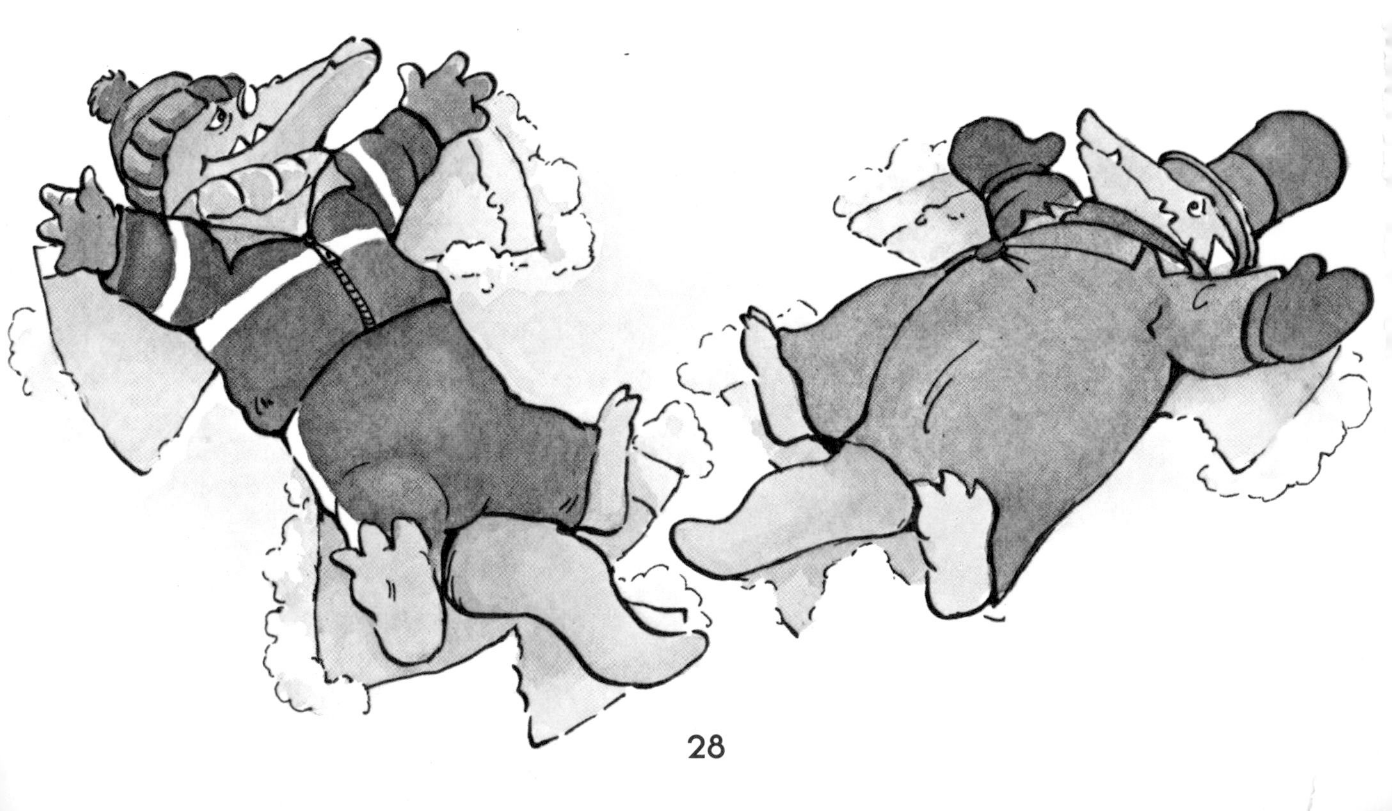

KYLE EATS SOME SOUP

One frosty morning Kyle made some soup. Hc put a BIG carrot and a LITTLE onion into a pot of boiling chicken broth.

He tossed in a LONG noodle and a SHORT green bean.

He found a THICK potato
and cut it into THIN slices.
He put them into the
broth and stirred it up.
He tasted it.

"Ouch!" Kyle cried.
"It's too HOT!"

Kyle turned off
the stove and let the soup sit.
He tasted it again.
"Aarrgh!" he cried.
"Now it's too COLD!"

Kyle was so angry he threw the soup UP into the air.

It came DOWN again.

Kyle threw the pot OUT the window,

but the snow came IN and covered his snout.

"Achoo!" Kyle sneezed. "I think I'm catching a cold."

He stepped OVER the mess on the floor

and curled up UNDER
the covers...
and soon fell asleep.

KYLE HAS A BIRTHDAY

One day a package arrived for Nasty Kyle the Crocodile. He opened it and found ten apples. There was a card, too. It said:

> Happy birthday, Kyle. I hope you like your present. I'll be visiting in a few days.
>
> See you soon,
> Your Uncle Miles

"Aarrgh!" said Kyle. "I hate birthdays. But I like Uncle Miles. Now, what can I make for his visit?"

First Kyle tried to make some apple sauce, but he went about it the wrong way. What a mess! All over the floor!

Kyle had nine apples left.

Next he tried baking apple pie. But the oven was too hot, and the crust turned black and burned.

Kyle had eight apples left.

"Apple brown betty is good," said Kyle. But he put in too much sugar. "Yuk," he said, "too sweet."

Kyle had seven apples left.

Kyle's banded mongoose stole one of the apples and ate it in the attic.

Kyle had six apples left.

Kyle tried to make some apple cider, but his press broke and the juice ran down his coat.

Kyle had only five apples left.

Kyle was so angry he took an apple and used it for target practice. By the time he was done the apple wasn't much good for anything.

Kyle now had four apples left.

One apple had a worm in it. Kyle threw it into the garbage.

Kyle had three apples left.

Then Kyle melted some caramel for a candied apple. But the caramel was so gooey it stuck to everything, and there wasn't much left for the apple.

Kyle had two apples left.

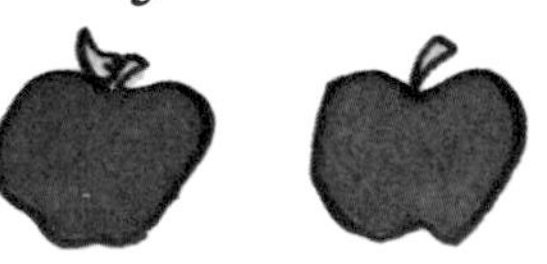

Just then the doorbell rang. It was Uncle Miles.

"Hello, Kyle," he said. "Did you get your birthday present?"

"Yes," said Kyle. "I tried to make something nice for us, but nothing turned out. I have only two apples left."

"That's all right," said Uncle Miles. "The very best way to eat apples is like this...with your favorite nephew."

Kyle and Uncle Miles sat under the maple tree in Kyle's backyard and watched the sun go down.

"Apples are delicious," said Uncle Miles.

"I still hate birthdays," said Kyle.